D0437951

This Ladybird Book belongs to:

_____

_____

_____

_____

This Ladybird retelling
by
Audrey Daly

Ladybird books are widely available, but in case of
difficulty may be ordered by post or telephone from:

Ladybird Books – Cash Sales Department
Littlegate Road Paignton Devon TQ3 3BE
Telephone 0803 554761

A catalogue record for this book is available
from the British Library

Published by Ladybird Books Ltd Loughborough Leicestershire UK
Ladybird Books Inc Auburn Maine 04210 USA

FAVOURITE TALES

Thumbelina

illustrated
by
PETULA STONE

based on the story by Hans Christian Andersen

Once upon a time there was a woman who longed to have a little girl of her own to love and care for. As time passed, and she had no children, she became very sad.

Then one day she heard of a wise old woman who could help, and she went to see her.

The wise old woman smiled. "Take this tiny seed and plant it in a flower pot," she said, "and you will have your little girl."

The woman took the seed home and planted it. Soon green shoots appeared, and a flower bud grew between them.

At last the bud opened out into a beautiful yellow flower. And right in the centre was a little girl, no bigger than the woman's thumb.

The woman looked down at the girl. "How pretty you are!" she said. "You are so small and dainty, I'm going to call you Thumbelina."

The woman was happy to have a little girl at last, and she took good care of Thumbelina.

Thumbelina was happy too. She sang songs in her soft, clear voice as she played on the kitchen table. At night she slept in a bed made from a tiny walnut shell.

Then one day a big toad heard
Thumbelina's singing and hopped in
through the window. "What a pretty
wife you would make for my son!" she
said. And she carried Thumbelina
away to the stream where she lived.

The toad left the tiny girl all alone on a lily leaf and went off to find her son.

Thumbelina didn't want to marry an ugly toad at all, but she didn't know how she could escape.

After a while some friendly fish came swimming by. "Please help me," Thumbelina begged. "The toad wants me to marry her son. I must find a way to escape!"

All the fish felt very sorry for Thumbelina. So they spent the whole day nibbling through the stem of the lily leaf, and at last Thumbelina was able to float away.

As she drifted down the stream, Thumbelina met a beautiful butterfly. It took her to a pleasant wood where she could make a home for herself.

Thumbelina was happy in the wood, eating the nuts and berries that she found, and playing with her friends the butterflies.

But soon the days grew colder. When winter came, it was harder for Thumbelina to find food. Her friends the butterflies disappeared, and she was alone.

Then one day Thumbelina met a friendly fieldmouse who was just going into her little house.

"I'm so hungry," Thumbelina said. "Please can you help me?"

The fieldmouse took pity on the girl. "Of course," she said. "You can stay with me in my warm house and share my food."

Thumbelina lived happily with the fieldmouse for a long time. But one day the fieldmouse said, "I can't keep you here much longer. Why don't you marry my friend the mole, who lives next door? He has a much bigger house than mine. And he will look after you next winter."

Thumbelina did not want to marry the mole. He lived under the ground and knew nothing of the sunny world outside.

Next day the mole visited Thumbelina.
"Please come and see where I live,"
he said.

Thumbelina did not want to hurt the mole's feelings, so she followed him into the tunnel that led to his dark underground home.

"Be careful," said the mole. "There is a dead bird just here."

Thumbelina saw that the bird was a
swallow. He was not dead, just very
cold and weak.

Thumbelina felt sorry for the swallow.
She covered him with dried leaves
and grass to keep him warm.

Thumbelina looked after the swallow all through the long, cold winter. By summer he was strong and well and ready to go back to his own home.

Thumbelina said goodbye to the swallow as he flew off with his friends. She was happy that he was well, but she knew that she would miss him. And she was sad to think that before the next winter came, she would have to marry the mole and live underground.

When summer ended, Thumbelina looked up at the sky for the last time with tears in her eyes. Birds were flying high overhead, and suddenly one of them swooped down to her. It was the swallow she had saved!

"I am going to a warm country," he told her. "Come with me."

Thumbelina was overjoyed. She climbed onto the swallow's back and flew with him to a faraway land where it was always summer.

This land was full of flowers. And inside every one lived a tiny person, just like Thumbelina!

"We are the Flower People," they said, "and this is your true home. We will call you Maia."

Maia loved her new home. Before long, she married the handsome Prince of the Flower People, and they lived happily ever after.

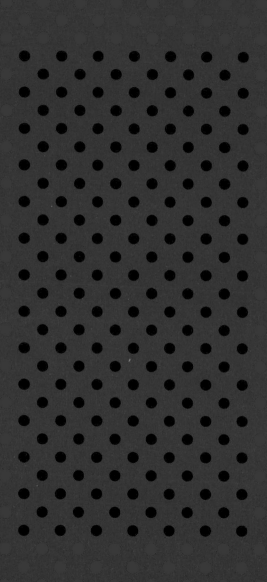